This Holiday Annual belongs to

....

Age...

My favourite engine is

....

EGMONT

We bring stories to life

First published in Great Britain 2011
by Egmont UK Limited
239 Kensington High Street, London W8 6SA

Thomas the Tank Engine & Friends™

CREATED BY BRITT ALLCROFT
Based on the Railway Series by the Reverend W Awdry
© 2011 Gullane (Thomas) LLC. A HIT Entertainment company.
Thomas the Tank Engine & Friends and Thomas & Friends
are trademarks of Gullane (Thomas) Limited.
Thomas the Tank Engine & Friends and Design is Reg. U.S. Pat. & Tm. Off.

HiT entertainment

ISBN 978 1 4052 5644 5
1 3 5 7 9 10 8 6 4 2
Printed in China

Contents

Welcome to Sodor

Hi, I'm Thomas!
Come and meet
my friends on
Sodor.

The Fat Controller
is in charge of the
Railway.

Percy is the youngest engine. He likes to deliver the mail.

Gordon is fast and strong. He pulls the Express.

Toby is a tram engine. He works on the Quarry line.

With his bright red coat, James is a Really Splendid Engine!

Edward is very kind and is a friend to everybody!

Henry is long and fast. But he does worry sometimes!

Rosie is a tank engine. She is great fun and likes to copy Thomas!

Harold works for the Sodor Search and Rescue Team.

Charlie loves adventures. He likes to help his friends.

Hiro is one of the strongest engines on the Railway.

Kevin is a funny crane. He works at the Sodor Steamworks.

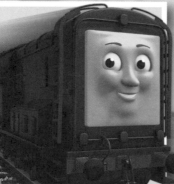

Diesel causes trouble sometimes. But he also likes to be a Really Useful Engine.

Spencer is a very smart and shiny engine. He's fast, too!

Cranky keeps things moving at Brendam Docks.

Peep! Peep!

Thomas is a very happy engine.
Colour him in as neatly as you can.

Thomas and James

Thomas has met James at an apple orchard. Which piece is missing from the jigsaw picture? Find the right sticker to complete the picture.

a

Answer: piece a is missing.

Toot! Toot!

Starting at number 1, join the dots to finish Bertie's picture.

Charlie's Adventure

Charlie has been busy chuffing around the Railway, but now he is lost. Which of the tracks will lead him back to The Fat Controller?

c

a **b**

Counting Time

How many pigs are in this picture with Thomas?

There are 2 pigs.

How many children are in this picture?

There are **3** children.

On the Farm

These close-ups can all be found in the big picture. Tick the circles when you have found them.

Thomas loves visiting farms!
Here he is picking up some
straw from Farmer McColl.

Shadow Match

Look at the engines and shadows.

1

2

3

Now draw a line to match each engine to its shadow.

b

a

1 - a
2 - c
3 - b

c

Answers: 1 a – Spencer, 2 c – Toby, 3 b – Hiro.

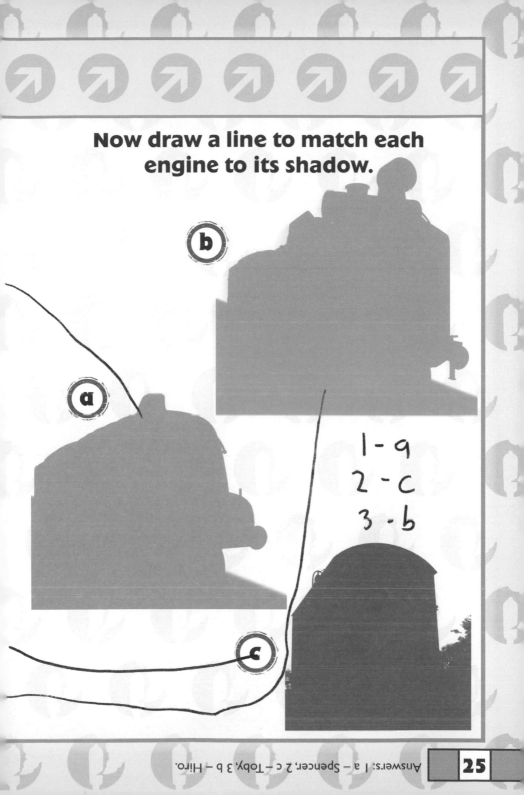

Spot the Difference

Gordon is the fastest and most powerful engine. These pictures look the same, but 5 things are different in picture 2.

1

Can you spot all the differences?

2

Answers: his buffer is missing; the sky is different; there is an extra tree; his funnel is longer; the red stripe is missing from his wheel arch.

Percy's Parcel

It was an exciting day on Sodor. It was Dowager Hatt's birthday and there was going to be a party.

Percy felt sad that he hadn't been given a special job to do. Kind Mavis tried to cheer Percy up.

Just then, The Fat Controller gave Percy a most important job!

"You must collect Dowager Hatt's birthday parcel from Brendam Docks," said The Fat Controller. "Then, you must deliver it to the party at Knapford Station," he said.

Percy beamed from buffer to buffer. And then he puffed off proudly.

Percy arrived at Brendam Docks. The parcel was very large and tied with a bright green bow. Percy wanted to show the parcel to Mavis.

Thomas was also at the Docks.

"Don't you have to take the parcel to Knapford Station?" asked Thomas.

But Percy did not want to listen to Thomas. He wanted to find Mavis.

Percy puffed away to the Quarry, proudly shunting the flatbed carrying the parcel.

At the Quarry, Percy found Mavis and Rocky working together. They were moving heavy slate.

"I'm sorry, Percy!" said Mavis. "I can't stop now, I'm too busy."

"I'll wait," replied Percy.

MAVIS

THE FFARQUHAR QUARRY CO.,LTD.

"Look out!" Rocky suddenly shouted. But it was too late. Rocky had dropped a heavy load of slate.

Mavis, Rocky and Percy were all covered in thick grey dust … and so was the parcel. Percy was upset.

Crash!

"Bubbling boilers!"
Percy exclaimed.
"Look at the parcel.
I must get it cleaned
at the wash down."

"Shouldn't you go
to Knapford, Percy?"
said Rocky.

Percy didn't want to
listen to Rocky. "I'll go
to Knapford as soon as I've
shown Mavis my special Special,"
said Percy.

And so, Percy steamed quickly away.

Percy puffed to the wash down. James was there as well.

Percy asked a Workman for a very good wash.

The man scrubbed and cleaned, and

water and soapy bubbles sprayed everywhere! Soon Percy was gleaming green again … but the birthday parcel was sopping wet!

"Bubbling boilers!" exclaimed Percy. "What am I going to do?" He then decided to go to the Steamworks. They could dry the parcel there.

"Shouldn't you go straight to Knapford, Percy?" said James.

Percy didn't want to listen to James. "I'll go to Knapford Station as soon as I've shown Mavis my special Special," replied Percy.

And so Percy chuffed quickly away.

Percy arrived at the Steamworks. Hot air
whooshed all over Percy and the parcel.
Percy was pleased … until he saw the
parcel. The paper was cracked and torn
and the green bow drooped.

Percy steamed sadly away. He had
spoiled Dowager Hatt's parcel. He slipped into
a siding near the junction, hidden by trees.

Just then, Mavis and Edward chuffed up to the junction. Mavis was pulling some brand new crates.

"I've just picked up these new crates from the Steamworks, Edward," explained Mavis.

Percy stopped feeling sad.

"A brand new crate is just what I need!" he peeped.

Percy raced back to the Steamworks. Victor was kind and gave Percy a bright red, brand new crate for the parcel.

Percy then puffed out of the Steamworks as proudly as can be!

At Knapford Station, The Fat Controller, Dowager Hatt, Mavis and the guests were waiting. Percy puffed in, pushing the bright red crate.

"Happy Birthday, Dowager Hatt!" peeped Percy. "Here's your very special present."

Dowager Hatt beamed. Workmen opened up the sides of the crate. They unwrapped lots of brown paper and the crinkly old red paper.

The present was a
beautiful portrait
of Dowager Hatt.

"Oh my!" gasped
Dowager Hatt.
"What a wonderful
surprise," she said,
giving The Fat
Controller a kiss.

"That's the most
special Special
I've ever seen,
Percy!" said Mavis.

Percy smiled from footplate to fender. He was
sure he was the happiest engine of all!

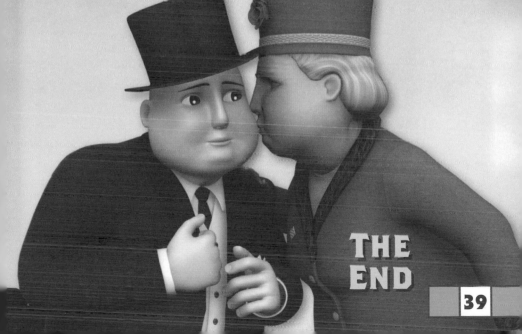

THE END

Here Comes Percy!

Percy is Thomas' best friend.
Colour him in as neatly as you can.

BUST MY BUFFERS
6 PERCY

Friends Together

Draw a line to match each shadow to its picture.

1 - b
2 - c
3 - d
4 - a

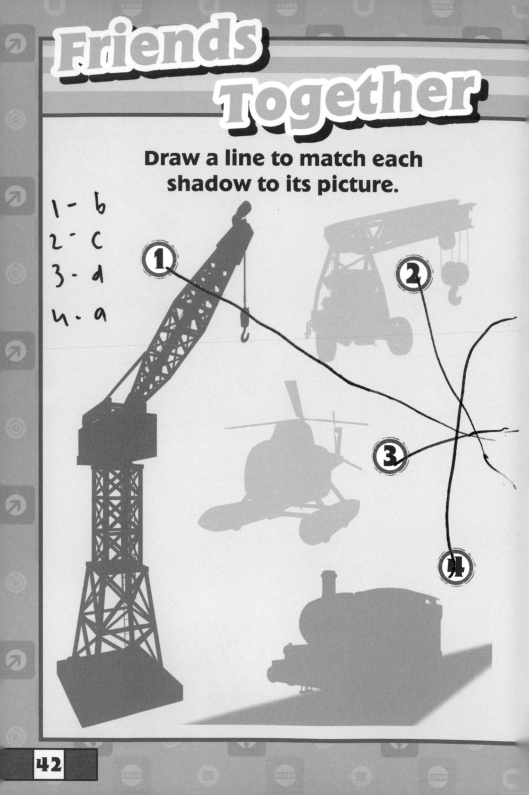

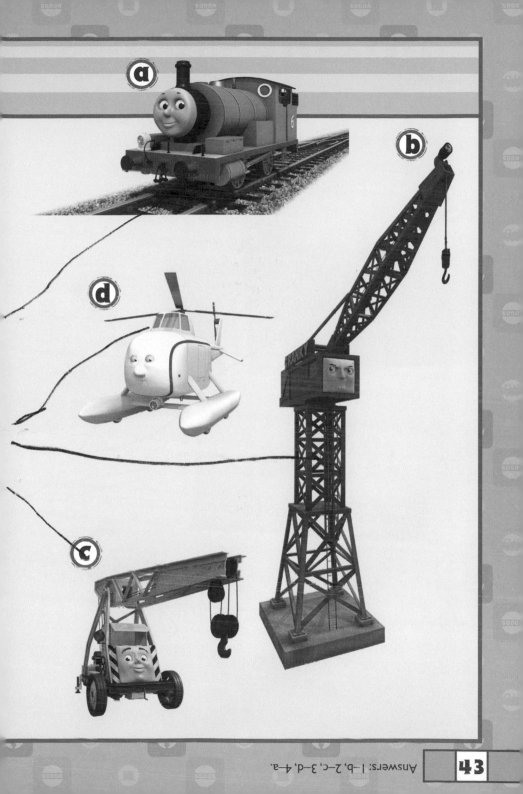

Matching Pairs

Look carefully at these pictures.
Now draw lines to match the
pairs of engines.

a

d

b

e

c

1 - b   5 - d
2 - e
3 - a
4 - c

Thomas and Charlie

Thomas and Charlie are chuffing alongside each other. Which piece is missing from the jigsaw picture? Find the right sticker to complete the picture.

a

c

b

Answer: piece b is missing.

Engine Numbers

Do you know what number each of these engines has painted on its side? Find the right number stickers and add them to the circles.

Answers: Thomas–1, Gordon–4.

All Aboard!

Annie is one of Thomas' carriages.
Starting at number 1, join the dots
to finish her picture.

Writing Time

Carefully copy over the lines to write the names of Hiro and Toby.

MASTER **51**
of the **RAILWAY**
The Island Of Sodor

Hiro

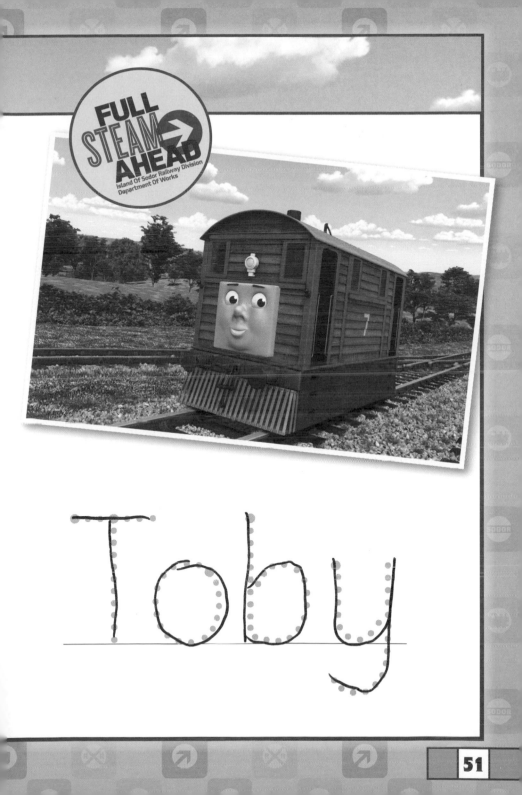

Toby's New Whistle

One day, Toby was at
the Steamworks. His bell
had stopped working.
It was covered in rust
and had to be left at
the Steamworks to be
cleaned.

Victor fitted Toby with a
new steam whistle. It felt
very strange for Toby.
It was much bigger than
his old bell. Toby was worried.

"I've never used a steam whistle
before," he said, sadly.

James chuffed into the Steamworks with The Fat Controller.

"That's a three-chime steam whistle," said James. "It's a loud and booming whistle!"

Toby was sad. He didn't like loud and booming noises. He liked the 'ding-a-ling' of his old bell.

The Fat Controller spoke. "Toby, you must collect Lady Hatt from Knapford," he said. "She's waiting!"

And so, Toby chuffed off to Knapford Station with his carriage Henrietta ... and his new whistle.

Toby chuffed
along slowly.

"I wish I had
my old bell
back," he said.

He puffed
carefully, hoping
that he wouldn't
need to use his whistle.
But before long, Gordon got stuck behind him.

"Out of my way, Toby, you old steam tram!" he
puffed. "You're making me late!"

They arrived at a junction, and Gordon was able
to steam ahead of Toby.

Toby came across some cows that had strayed onto the tracks. He put on his brakes.

"Go away cows, please!" Toby said.

But the cows took no notice. They were busy mooing and chewing. Toby knew that he should blow his steam whistle ... but he was too scared.

Toby steamed backwards down the track to find help. He saw some Workmen in a field, nearby.

"Excuse me!" Toby shouted. "Hello! Hello!"

But the men didn't hear Toby. And so he huffed back to the cows on the tracks. They were still mooing and chewing.

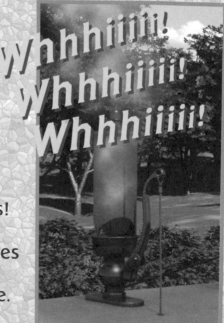

Whhhiiiii!
Whhhiiiii!
Whhhiiiii!

Just then, Toby heard another engine. It was Thomas, and he was heading towards the cows! Toby knew that he had to be brave. He closed his eyes and blew into his new three-chime steam whistle.

It was the loudest whistle anyone had ever heard! As soon as Thomas heard it, he put on his brakes.

"Cinders and ashes!" exclaimed Thomas.

Thomas screeched to a halt, sparks flying. He had stopped just in time!

Screeeech!

"Thank you, Toby!" said Thomas.

Toby felt very proud. He was pleased he'd used his new whistle. Thomas' crew moved the cows off the track. Suddenly, Toby remembered Lady Hatt!

"I must puff to Knapford quickly!" Toby said.

Thomas left with Toby and they puffed along the tracks. They were waiting at a red signal when they saw The Fat Controller. He was very cross.

"Toby," said The Fat Controller, "Lady Hatt waited for a very long time. Gordon is taking her home."

Toby was upset. "I'm sorry, Sir ..." said Toby.

And then Toby stopped. He could see something on the track ahead.

"There's a fallen tree on the tracks!" said Toby. Everybody looked at the tree. And further up the track, they could see Gordon steaming towards it!

"Don't worry, Sir," said Toby to The Fat Controller. "I know just what to do!"

Toby bubbled his boiler and pumped his pistons. He then blew into his three-chime steam whistle as loudly as he could.

Gordon braked and screeched to a halt. He looked up and saw Toby.

Whhhiiii!
Whhhiiii!
Whhhiiii!

"Toby!" Gordon said. "For a steam tram, you have a lot of puff! Thank you for blowing your whistle so loudly."

Just then, Lady Hatt popped her head out of Gordon's carriage and waved.

"Well done, Toby!" Lady Hatt called.

Toby couldn't have felt more proud.

Later on, Toby was back at the Steamworks. Victor had mended his old bell. It glistened and gleamed. Kevin lifted out the steam whistle and fitted Toby's old bell back into place.

"Did you like the three-chime steam whistle?" Victor asked.

"The whistle was Really Useful," replied Toby.

"You can keep it if you like," said Victor.

"No, thank you," said Toby. "My own bell is best of all!" he smiled.

And Toby was so happy, he gave a little 'ding-a-ling' on his bell!

THE END

A Really Splendid Engine

James is very proud of his fine red coat!
Colour him in as neatly as you can.

MIND MY PAINTWORK

⑤ JAMES

Who's who?

Draw lines to match the characters to their names and descriptions.

1

EMILY

My name is Emily.
I am a beautiful green
engine with shiny
brass fittings.

2

VICTOR

My name is Victor.
I run the Sodor
Steamworks.

3

CHARLIE

My name is Charlie.
I am a small engine who
likes to have lots of fun.

1 - b
2 - c
3 - a

Speedy Spencer

Show Spencer the fastest way through the maze. Then add the sticker of The Fat Controller.

Start

Finish

Answer:

Henry Spotting

One of these pictures of Henry is different from the rest. Can you spot the odd one out?

A Blooming Mess!

MAVIS

THE FFARQUHAR QU...

You can read this story! When you
see the pictures of the friends,
say their names.

KEY

Thomas

Emily

Toby

James

Mavis

Edward

Knapford Station was being

decorated! was sent to the

Quarry to collect some slate for the

new roof. had to collect some

flowers from Maithwaite Station.

As she puffed along, she passed

. He was delivering wood.

Then she passed . He was

delivering paint. Further along the

track,  saw on a bridge.

"Hello!" she peeped. But didn't say hello back. thought that she must be feeling sad. Later on, pulled into Maithwaite Station. There were lots of pretty flowers for her to collect. "I could take some to at the Quarry!" she thought. "That would cheer her up." And so didn't puff back to

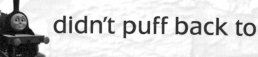

KEY

 Thomas   Emily   Toby

Knapford with the flowers. She took

them to the Quarry instead. When

she arrived, wasn't there.

 left a flatbed of flowers

for her at the entrance. Suddenly,

there was a loud **CRASH!**

 had arrived, and he'd

crashed straight into the flatbed of

flowers! "Look out!" peeped .

James   Mavis   Edward

"Those flowers are for , to make her happy." then left another flatbed of flowers by the slate hopper. Meanwhile, had arrived. He reversed towards the hopper, with a truck. There was another loud **CRASH!**

 and his truck had bumped into the second flatbed of flowers,

74

which banged into the first flatbed,

and pushed into a buffer.

"Cinders and ashes!" peeped .

"Bust my buffers!" wheezed

 . Just then,  pulled

into the Quarry. She was horrified.

"What has happened?" she huffed.

 gasped. "The Quarry is in a

terrible mess, and it's all my fault!"

James   Mavis   Edward

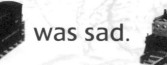 told that she'd brought

some flowers because she thought

 was sad. explained

that she wasn't sad. She hadn't said

'hello' because she'd been busy

thinking about all the jobs she had

to do. felt very silly. She

asked what would make her

happy. "I would like the Quarry to

be tidy and all the engines to be

Really Useful," she replied.

felt pleased. She now knew exactly

how to make  happy! First,

she helped . He was stuck

under the hopper, covered in slate

dust.  buffered up to

and pulled him away from the slate

hopper.  then biffed and

 James  Mavis  Edward

bashed the flatbeds away from the

hopper. went to collect his

trucks. puffed away with

his slate truck.  pulled up to

. "Now I want you to deliver

the flowers to Knapford Station," she

said, kindly. And so,  chuffed

happily away. She soon arrived

at Knapford Station. Workmen

unloaded the flatbeds. The flowers

looked very pretty.  puffed

by and said, "Now I am very happy.

Those flowers look wonderful!" And

this made happy, too!

THE END

James   Mavis   Edward

Engine Match

Do you know the names of these
Really Useful Engines?
Find the name stickers and place each
one next to the correct engine.

Percy

Thomas

Emily

Colouring Time

**Gordon is a very fast blue engine.
Colour him in as neatly as you can.**

To the Rescue!

Cranky's crane arm is breaking! Use your stickers to show The Fat Controller and Harold rushing to help.

Engine Names

Look carefully at these engine names and pictures. Now draw a line to match each engine to its name.

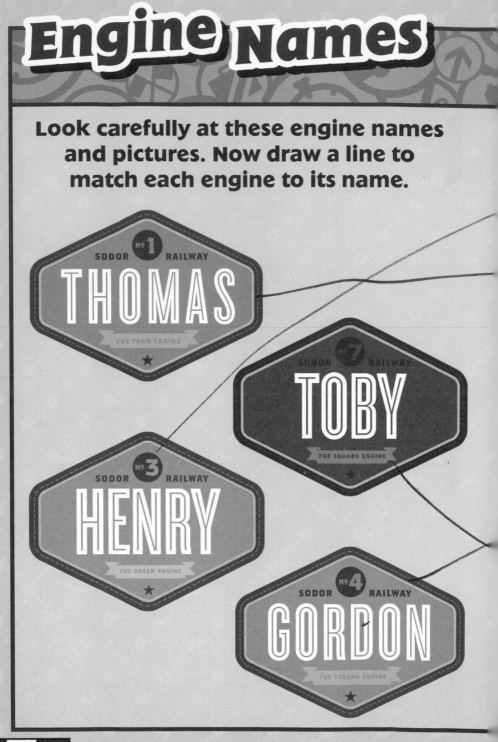

SODOR № 1 RAILWAY
THOMAS
THE TANK ENGINE

SODOR № 7 RAILWAY
TOBY
THE SQUARE ENGINE

SODOR № 3 RAILWAY
HENRY
THE GREEN ENGINE

SODOR № 4 RAILWAY
GORDON
THE STRONG ENGINE

Here Comes Bertie!

Bertie is a very happy bus. He is good friends with Thomas. Colour him in, using the little picture as a guide.

You could add some stickers, too!

Home Time

These close-ups can all be found in the big picture. Tick the circles when you have found them.

It's the end of another busy day, and Thomas is steaming home.

Tidmouth Sheds

Thomas has got lost on his way home. Can you help show him the way back to Tidmouth Sheds?

Start

Finish

Answer:

Goodbye!

"Goodbye, everyone. Come and join us on Sodor again soon!"

Get 20% off
Thomas Personalised Books!

'You'
and the Birthday Surprise

THOMAS & FRIENDS

Free Delivery!

'You'
and the Christmas Rescue

THOMAS & FRIENDS

Available in 2 Editions with 20% Off!*

Creating your personalised adventure is really easy!

Simply enter your child's name, create their picture by choosing from a range of cute features and these will automatically be entered into the rest of the story book! If you like what you see, claim 20% off by entering the **discount code U11-TAFPOD** at the checkout, then we'll deliver it direct to your door for free!